D0116550

Katy Duck Makes a Friend

By Alyssa Satin Capucilli · Illustrated by Henry Cole

Ready-to-Read

Simon Spotlight
New York London Toronto Sydney New Delhi

For my new friends, Molly Isabelle, Sydney Reese,
Samantha Hazel, Odessa Naomi, and Amalya Eliza!—A. S. C.

For my buddy Caroline!—H. C.

SIMON SPOTLIGHT
An imprint of Simon & Schuster Children's Publishing Division
1230 Avenue of the Americas, New York, New York 10020

Manufactured in the United States of America 0312 LAK
10 9 8 7 6 5 4 3 2
Library of Congress Cataloging-in-Publication Data
Capucilli, Alyssa Satin, 1957-
Katy Duck makes a friend / by Alyssa Satin Capucilli ; illustrated by Henry Cole. — 1st ed.
p. cm. — (Ready-to-read)
Summary: When Katy Duck, who loves to dance, meets her new neighbor Ralph, it turns out that he
loves rough and tumble games and the two of them must figure out a way to play together.
ISBN 978-1-4424-1976-6 (pbk.)
ISBN 978-1-4424-1977-3 (hardcover)
[1. Dance—Fiction. 2. Play—Fiction. 3. Ducks—Fiction. 4. Dogs—Fiction. 5. Neighbors—Fiction.]
I. Cole, Henry, 1955- ill. II. Title.
PZ7.C179Km 2012
[E]—dc23
2011020268
ISBN 978-1-4424-4719-6 (eBook)

Katy Duck loves to
dance.
“Tra-la-la.
Quack! Quack!”

Katy Duck loves to dance
with her brother, Emmett.
“Tra-la-la.
Quack! Quack!”

Katy leaps and twirls.
Emmett jumps and
bumps.

Soon Mrs. Duck says,
"It is time for a nap,
Emmett."

“Tra-la-la. Boo-hoo,”
says Katy.
“Who can I dance with
now?”

Just then the doorbell rings! "That must be our new neighbor," says Mrs. Duck.

“I hope our new neighbor

loves to dance,”

says Katy Duck.

Katy Duck opens
the door.
She does her
best curtsy!

"Hello! My name is Katy Duck. I love to dance!

Tra-la-la!
Quack! Quack!"

"I am Ralph.
I love things that
go fast."

“I love cars.

I love airplanes.

I love rocket ships.

Zip! Zoom! Whoo-oo-sh!”

Katy Duck looks to her left.

"Do you like to dance?" asks Katy.

Ralph looks to his right. “Do you like things that go fast?” he asks.

Katy and Ralph look down. "There must be something we both like to do," says Katy Duck.

“But what?” asks Ralph.

Katy and
Ralph
think and
think.

They think
and think
some more.

"I know!" says Katy Duck. She flaps her arms up and down.

Katy zips.

Katy zooms.

“Look at me, Ralph! I am an airplane! Tra-la-la. Quack! Whee!” says Katy Duck.

"10-9-8-7-6-5-4-3-2-1 . . .

BLAST OFF!" shouts

Ralph.

"I am a rocket ship."

"Me too!
BLAST OFF!"
says Katy
Duck.

"This is fun!"
says Ralph.

They zip and zoom.
They whirl and twirl.

"How I love
to dance,"
says Katy
Duck.

"Especially with a new
friend like you, Ralph.
Tra-la-la.
Quack! Quack!"